Haffertee's First Christmas

Haffertee is a soft-toy hamster. Ma Diamond made him for her little girl, Yolanda (Diamond Yo), when her real pet hamster died.

In this book – the fourth in the series – Haffertee tangles with a box of decorations, becomes a Christmas Detective and unravels a number of clues which lead him to a Happy Christmas. Through stars and a cowshed, cards and carols, Haffertee discovers what Christmas is all about.

The charm of the stories lies in the funny, lovable character of Haffertee himself, and in the special place God has in the affections of Diamond Yo and her family.

The
Diamond
Family

Fran   Ma

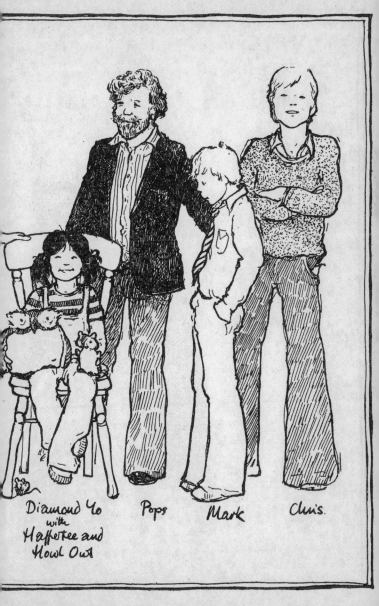

Diamond Yo
with
Hafferkee and
Howl Out

Pops

Mark

Chris.

Haffertee's First Christmas

Haffertee's First Christmas

By Janet and John Perkins
Illustrations by Gillian Gaze

A LION PAPERBACK

Copyright © 1977 Janet and John Perkins

Published by
Lion Publishing
Icknield Way, Tring, Herts, England
ISBN 0 85648 493 8
Albatross Books
PO Box 320, Sutherland, NSW 2232, Australia
ISBN 0 86760 375 5

First edition 1977
Second edition 1979
This edition 1982

Cover picture and illustrations by Gillian Gaze
Copyright © 1977 Lion Publishing

Printed and bound in Great Britain by
Collins, Glasgow

Contents

It all began when Yo's pet hamster died. To cheer her up, Ma Diamond made a ginger-and-white soft-toy hamster. The new Haffertee Hamster Diamond proved to be quite a character – inquisitive, funny and lovable. From his home in Yo's bedroom – shared with his friend Howl Owl and a strange collection of toys – he set out to explore Hillside House and meet the family: Ma and Pops Diamond and Yo's older brothers and sister, Chris, Fran and Mark. His adventures in the house and garden, and the World Outside are told in four books of stories: *Haffertee Hamster Diamond*, *Haffertee Hamster's New House*, *Haffertee Goes Exploring* and *Haffertee's First Christmas*.

Haffertee Gets in a Tangle

Haffertee Hamster Diamond stood in Yo's doorway. Coloured paper and tinsel tumbled all over the floor on the landing. Gold stars and silver stars and red stars twinkled everywhere. There were paper chains and streamers and hanging paper bells. And right in the middle was Yo's brother Mark. Haffertee pushed bravely on into the confusion.

'Whatever are you doing?' he asked. One of the gold stars was stuck between his legs.

'Sorry, Haffertee,' said Mark. 'I didn't know you were in Yo's room. I was sent up to find the Decorations Box and sort everything into piles.'

Haffertee stood looking at the tangle. 'What do you want all this for?' he asked at last.

'Well,' said Mark. 'It's time to decorate the house. Will you help me sort all these things out?'

Haffertee was puzzled. Whatever did Mark mean about decorating the house? Still, it would be fun to help.

'I'll try,' he said and, stepping carefully among the piles of decorations, he began to untangle some of the twists.

It was a long time before everything was properly sorted. Mark put the piles tidily in the Decorations Box, picked it up and set off downstairs. Haffertee trotted close behind. Mark was putting the box down on the floor as Haffertee slipped past him into the kitchen.

'Look out!' shouted a very loud voice. There was just time to 'Look Out' and 'Look Round' before a green tree with spikes came rushing towards him.

Haffertee jumped back against the wall and let the tree go by. It shot past him to the corner of the room and settled down on top of a small table. The branches parted and Pops Diamond's head appeared.

'Sorry, Haffertee,' he spluttered. 'But I must get this tree ready this morning.' And he hurried back into the garden.

Haffertee was just getting over being rushed at by a spiky tree when Fran Diamond poked her head round the back door.

'Is Mark in there?' she whispered.

'No!' replied Haffertee. 'He has gone up to his room.'

'Good,' said Fran, running quickly across the

kitchen and up to her own room. As she passed, Haffertee could see that she was holding a parcel behind her back. It was wrapped in sparkling red and gold paper.

'What's that, Fran?' asked Haffertee, but he was wasting his breath. She was already halfway up the stairs.

Then Chris Diamond burst in. 'Great! Great! I've got it fixed at last,' he shouted. Then *he* was gone, leaping up the stairs two at a time.

Things were happening so fast, Haffertee felt all in a whirl. He took a deep breath, closed his eyes and counted up to ten very slowly. It was a trick Howl Owl had taught him. The thing to do when flustered.

'One . . . two . . . three . . . four . . . five . . .

six . . . seven . . . eight . . . nine . . . ten.' That was better!

'Whatever is going on?' he asked nobody in particular, as Ma Diamond rustled into the kitchen with a huge white bag made of thick paper. In large red letters on the side Haffertee could read the words HAPPY CHRISTMAS.

'Hello, Haffertee,' she said, a little out of breath. 'I am glad I've found this.'

She held up the bag for Haffertee to see, then walked over to the corner. She put the bag under the tree.

Haffertee watched with a puzzled look on his face. 'Whatever . . .' he began. But he didn't get time to finish his question.

'I must get on with the dinner now,' Ma said, and she started opening the oven door.

So Haffertee knew he would have to wait. The kitchen was no place for questions when Ma was getting dinner ready. He started back to Yo's room.

As he went up the stairs, Haffertee heard Chris strumming away on his guitar. He was singing a very happy little song. The bedroom door was closed, so the words were rather muffled. But when it came to the chorus Chris sang extra loudly. Haffertee could hear quite clearly.

'Baby born.
Jesus child.
Hear the angels sing.
Baby born.
God's own style.
Little Jesus King.'

It was such a cheerful song that Haffertee stood quite still to listen.

'Puzzles and yet more puzzles,' he thought. Decorations and a spiky tree. A secret parcel wrapped in special paper. Happy Christmas – whatever was that? And a song about a baby – little Jesus King!

Haffertee couldn't make it out. He felt all in a tangle himself!

The Christmas Detective

'Beep! Beep!' said Yo, as she came up the stairs carefully carrying a small step-ladder.

For the second time that day Haffertee tucked himself against the wall. Yo squeezed past.

'Will you help me decorate our room, Haffertee?' she said, standing the steps firmly in the corner of the bedroom.

'Decorations again,' thought Haffertee as he watched her struggling to pin the end of a streamer somewhere up near the ceiling. It looked a bit dangerous. But if he helped perhaps Yo would answer his questions.

Between them they soon had the room looking bright and gay. Then they stopped for a rest, and sat admiring the paper chains and streamers. The room seemed to chuckle with fun.

Haffertee turned to Yo. It seemed a good moment. 'What *is* it all about, Yo?' he asked.

'What is what all about?' said Yo.

'You know,' said Haffertee. 'Dressing up the bedroom like this, bringing a tree into the kitchen, and everyone doing such odd things. What is it all about?'

Of course! It was Haffertee's first Christmas. No wonder he was looking so puzzled. It had been such an exciting morning that Yo hadn't thought to explain. She picked Haffertee up and poggled his ears. He snuggled into her neck.

'It's like this, Haffertee,' she said. 'We're all getting ready for Christmas, and Christmas is a very special birthday.'

'Oh!' said Haffertee. 'Like Fran's birthday? That was lovely.'

'Yes,' said Yo. 'You know, when it's someone's birthday we give them presents and try to make it a happy day.'

'Whose birthday is it this time, then?' asked Haffertee.

'Ahh!' said Yo. 'Someone very special. He has friends all over the world who love him and want to make him happy. His name is Jesus Christ. That's why we call his birthday Christmas.' Haffertee was all ears.

'Jesus said that if we're kind to other people it's

like being kind to him.' Yo went on. 'That's what makes his birthday such fun. We try to make everyone happy, so that Jesus has a happy birthday, too.'

So *that* was it, thought Haffertee. Pretty decorations, secret parcels and a HAPPY CHRISTMAS – all for Jesus' birthday. And Jesus was a friend of Yo's. Jesus Christ . . . Little Jesus King. What a lot of names!

'Is it Christmas today, Yo?' Haffertee asked.

'No! No! Haffertee. There are lots more lovely things to come first. Come on, let's go down to the kitchen.'

Chris and Fran were both there, stirring the mincemeat mixture ready for the first batch of mince pies. Ma was rolling out the pastry. Yo went over to help.

She turned to speak to Haffertee. But he had disappeared. Yo looked more carefully, and burst out laughing at what she saw. Haffertee had fallen head-first into the big white paper bag under the tree. He was trying to see what a HAPPY CHRISTMAS looked like!

Suddenly a head and one paw emerged. An excited Haffertee Hamster climbed out, waving a white envelope.

'It's for me. It's for me,' he shrieked. And sure enough the little white envelope had Haffertee's name printed clearly on one side in bright blue letters.

Everyone gathered round to see. It was very quiet in the kitchen as Haffertee opened the envelope and looked inside. He pulled out a small round

18

cardboard badge with a string tied through a hole in the top. On it was written

HAFFERTEE HAMSTER DIAMOND: CHRISTMAS DETECTIVE

Ma looked at Chris and Chris looked at Fran and Fran looked at Yo. And then they all turned and looked at the door, where Pops was standing smiling at them all.

'This is some of your work, isn't it?' said Ma. 'You'd better explain.'

Pops laughed.

'Well,' he said. 'Ever since this morning when I came in with the Christmas tree Haffertee has been all in a tangle. I thought we'd make him a Christmas Detective, so that he could sort the tangle out. He'll need some clues, of course, and everyone must help. Put your badge on now, Haffertee, ready for the first clue.'

Haffertee put his head through the string loop. The badge hung right down on his tummy. He bent forward to admire it, feeling most important. Haffertee Hamster Diamond: Christmas Detective!

'Listen now,' said Pops, and he read out the first clue:

'Watch out when the holly comes
And copper pots appear.
Then look round for a cowshed
With special people there.'

Haffertee repeated the lines till he knew them by heart. He was a Christmas Detective. He was going to find out all about the Happy Christmas.

Holly and copper pots . . . He could hardly wait to get started.

Haffertee and the Cowshed

There was an argument going on in the kitchen. The voices were beginning to get very loud indeed.

'I don't want to clean the copper. It's my turn to go and fetch the holly,' said Yo, sharply. 'You did it last year.'

'No. I didn't,' said Mark, just as sharply. 'You did.'

It was Fran who stopped the argument by calling down from her room. 'I'll clean the copper for you, Mum. Let those two go and get the holly together.'

Mark and Yo grinned at one another and went to put on their shoes and coats.

'Don't forget your gloves,' said Ma. 'Remember the prickles!'

Haffertee rubbed his badge. 'Can I come too?' he said, and quickly snuggled into Yo's pocket as she and Mark set off. He was following his first clue.

The sun was bright but the air was very cold. Mark and Yo knew just where the best holly grew and the three of them were soon home again with an armful of shiny green holly and a few red berries showing here and there.

'We had a job to find any with berries on this

year, Mum,' said Mark.

'Never mind,' said Ma. 'The leaves are lovely on their own.'

Mark and Yo put their bunches of holly down carefully on the kitchen floor.

Haffertee jumped out of Yo's pocket. She hadn't let him pick the holly in case he pricked himself. Now was his chance to touch the shiny leaves. He put out a paw . . . and quickly jumped back!

'Ouch!' he cried, sucking his pricked paw. 'What are they going to do with prickly stuff like this?'

Fran had nearly finished polishing the old copper tea urn and the coffee pot. They sparkled and shone.

'That *is* lovely,' said Ma. 'I do like my copper bright and shiny. But I don't like doing all that rubbing. Thank you, Fran. You've done a grand job.'

Haffertee stood in front of the coffee pot. It was so shiny he could see himself. He turned this way and

that. What a funny shape he looked – all short and fat. He couldn't help chuckling. .

'Right,' said Ma. 'That's the copper and the holly. Now all we need are the little figures. Yo! There's a green shoe-box under the stairs marked *"Nativity"*. Would you get it for me please?'

While Yo searched the cupboard under the stairs, Haffertee helped Ma cover the table with red crêpe paper. Then he stood well back while she arranged the holly: large sprays in the huge copper tea urn, smaller ones for the copper coffee pot. Still more holly lay on the red paper.

Haffertee moved closer as Ma put lots of little coloured light bulbs in the holly. A flick of the switch and all the bulbs twinkled among the holly and shone back from the copper.

'How lovely,' thought Haffertee. 'Howl Owl must see this.' And he scampered upstairs. Howl Owl was dozing on his shelf in Yo's room.

'Howl! Howl! Wake up, Howl! Come quickly and see what Ma has made.'

Howl opened first one eye, then the other. Silently, he spread his wings and flew slowly downstairs while Haffertee tumbled over himself in his hurry not to miss what was going on.

'Humph!' said Howl, settling on the back of a chair. 'Humph!' And that was all he said. But he looked . . . and looked . . . and looked . . . and smiled.

'Now then,' said Ma. 'Let's get started.'

'That's funny,' said Haffertee to himself. 'I thought we'd finished.'

But Yo was back now, sitting on the floor with

23

the green shoe-box open in front of her. Haffertee went over and peeped in.

'Baby Jesus first,' said Yo, as she carefully picked up a tiny figure of a baby from the shoe-box. She settled the baby in a funny-shaped cot and handed him to Ma.

Haffertee pricked up his ears again, remembering Chris's song, 'Baby Jesus . . . Little Jesus King?'

Yo was reaching into the box again. She found the figures of Mary and Joseph and Ma put them close to the baby. Two cows, a goat and a donkey were standing nearby – all looking at Jesus.

'What do you want next, Ma?' said Yo.

'The shepherds were the first to come and see him,' said Ma. Yo found some sheep and their shepherds. One of them was carrying a tiny lamb.

'And here are the three kings,' said Yo, showing them to Haffertee and Howl. 'They wore wonderful robes and brought presents for Jesus.'

Ma took the little figures and put them in their places and then stood back.

'There's something missing,' she said. Then she remembered what it was. She fetched a picture of a cowshed which Yo had drawn and stood it up behind all the figures.

'The cowshed! The cowshed!' shouted Haffertee in great excitement. 'That's the clue. A cowshed . . . and special people.' He looked at the baby and Mary and Joseph, the shepherds and the kings. They were certainly special people! But why were they all in a cowshed?' He looked down at his Christmas Detective Badge. Detectives asked questions. That was

24

how they found things out. Howl Owl had told him all about being a Detective.

'Was Jesus born in a cowshed, then?' he asked.

'Yes,' said Howl. 'And there was a big brown owl sitting in the rafters.'

'Was there really?' said Haffertee.

'Weller . . . P'raps,' said Howl, with a smile.

'Why wasn't Jesus born in a proper house?' asked Haffertee.

'Weller . . .' said Howl again, very slowly.

But it was Yo who gave Haffertee his answer.

'There wasn't any room for them in the village inn, Haffertee, so they had to sleep in the stable out at the back. And Jesus was born there that night. His mother wrapped him up warmly and put him to sleep on some straw in a manger. That was where the shepherds found him. They were as surprised as you.'

Haffertee stood still, looking at the figures in the cowshed. Yo began to sing . . .

'Away in a manger, no crib for a bed
The little Lord Jesus laid down his sweet head.
The stars in the bright sky looked down where
he lay,
The little Lord Jesus asleep on the hay.'

'What a lovely song,' said Haffertee, slowly when Yo had finished.

'It's my favourite carol,' said Yo. 'You've done some good detecting, Haffertee. Here is a picture of the special people in the cowshed. Keep it carefully in your Very Own Box. You'll need it again. It's time for the next clue now, so listen carefully.

When you decorate the tree
With stars and golden bells,
That is the time the angel comes
– listen to what he tells.'

The Tree and the Angel

Haffertee and Yo came trundling into the kitchen.
Ma was very busy. Haffertee and Yo were looking
for something to do.

'Can we help you?' asked Yo.

Ma put both her hands to her head.

'Just keep out of the kitchen and let me get on,' she
said rather fiercely and all in a hurry. Then . . .
'Yo, my love, I'm sorry. There *is* something you can
do. Will you two decorate the tree for me?'

'Oh! Yes please,' squealed Haffertee, excitedly.
'This is the time the angel comes,' he thought,
remembering the second clue, and looking again at
his Christmas Detective badge.

'We'll try, Ma,' said Yo.

'Then go and fetch the Decorations Box while I finish putting the groceries away,' said Ma.

When the two of them came back, Ma fixed lots of coloured light bulbs to the branches of the spiky tree. Then she switched them on.

'Ahhh!' they all said, as the lights came on.

'Ohhh!' said Haffertee, as the lights suddenly went out again.

'Sorry,' said Ma. 'But I must switch them off while you hang things on the tree. Now I must get on.' And she turned back to the oven and the dinner she was cooking.

Haffertee knew just where to find the glass baubles, the silver thread, the plastic icicles and the glitter. After all, he had helped Mark sort them out. He handed them one by one to Yo, and she fixed everything on the tree. It was *beautiful*.

Ma was delighted. 'Now you can put the angel on top,' she said.

'May I really?' said Yo, hardly believing her ears. One of the grown-ups usually did that.

'I'll fetch him,' said Ma.

'The angel,' thought Haffertee. 'The angel I have to listen to?'

Ma lifted the lovely angel from the box, and Haffertee understood Yo's excitement. He was a wonderful angel. But not a talking angel, surely?

Yo was already on the steps when Ma handed him up to her. Everyone held his breath until the angel was safely fixed at the very top of the tree.

'Yo, tell Haffertee what the angel said to the

shepherds who were out on the hills at Bethlehem looking after their sheep,' said Ma.

Yo came down the steps slowly and turned to Haffertee. She cleared her throat, to make the words sound really important.

'"Don't be afraid," the angel said, "I've got some wonderful news for the whole world. King Jesus has been born in the village tonight." Do you know what happened then, Haffertee?'

The little hamster shook his head. So that was it, he thought. A real angel, not a talking Christmas tree angel.

'Hundreds of other angels came into the sky,' Yo went on. Then she turned to Ma. 'Can we have our angels on now, Mummy?'

Ma switched on the Christmas tree lights.

'See all those lights, Haffertee?' said Yo. Haffertee nodded. 'I think of the real Christmas angels when I see them. That night all the angels shouted to the world . . . "God is wonderful. He gives peace to everyone who loves him." '

Haffertee stood still, looking at the pretty lights and the shining angel right at the very top of the tree. Yo had explained to him about God – he was the Great Maker. Haffertee was wishing he'd been out on the hills with the shepherds and the sheep on the night the angels came. He could have asked them all about little Jesus King.

He was still thinking about that at bedtime. He snuggled down warmly in his Very Own Box. The bedroom curtains weren't drawn and through the door he could see the sky full of stars. Haffertee's eyes closed.

He could see the angels . . . He could hear them singing . . .

Stars at Every Window

In the morning Howl shook Haffertee awake. 'A message,' he said. 'An important message. Wake up!'

Haffertee rubbed the sleep from the eyes. Propped up by his feet was a card. It had a picture of an angel on it.

'Keep it with the cowshed picture,' Howl said. 'That's two clues and two pictures. You've listened to the angel. Now it's time for the third clue.'

Haffertee reached for his Christmas Detective badge and put it on. Solemnly Howl Owl began to recite:

'Look out for a star next.
Yo will tell you why.
How it shone for wise men.
In the eastern sky.'

A star! That was an easy one, Haffertee thought. The stars were just outside the window. He'd seen them only last night. He peered out. But to his dismay there wasn't a star to be seen. Where had they gone?

Howl Owl gave a little hoot of laughter and explained. Haffertee sighed. He would have to wait all day till it was dark again to see his star.

Diamond Yo had been working hard at her desk for a long time. She was making some sort of model.

At last she got up from her chair, stretched, and went downstairs. Haffertee heard the back door slam and footsteps going down the garden path. Yo had gone to the beach for some fresh air.

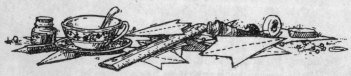

Haffertee decided to see what she'd been making. He climbed carefully up on to the desk and looked around. There was a pencil and a rubber and a ruler and several pieces of cardboard. Haffertee picked up one of them. It didn't look like anything in particular. He put the first piece down and picked up another one. But that wasn't any better. It was all very puzzling.

As he stood there, trying to think what it was, Yo came back.

'What are you doing on my desk?' she said.

'I wanted to see what you were doing,' said Haffertee. 'You don't mind do you?'

'Of course not,' said Yo. 'Did you guess what it was?'

'No,' said Haffertee.

'I'll show you, then,' said Yo. And she picked up the pieces of cardboard and put them together.

'There,' she said. 'Can you see what it is now?'

Haffertee looked at it closely. He twisted his head

32

a little to one side and then to the other. He moved back a few steps to get a better look. But he still couldn't guess what it was.

'It's a star,' said Yo. 'But it isn't finished yet. I'm going to glue the pieces together and spray it with some silver paint. Then it will be a lovely star.'

Haffertee felt excited. Perhaps *this* was his star. He must ask some detective questions.

'What do you want a cardboard star for?' he began.

'I always make a big one every year,' explained Yo. 'We hang it in the front room for everyone to see.'

'Why?' asked Haffertee, thinking what a good detective he was learning to be.

'Well,' said Yo, 'when Jesus was born, God put a very special star in the sky to mark the place where he was. It started in the east and moved across the sky for a long way until it came and stopped just above that cowshed in Bethlehem. It guided some wise men all the way from their own country to the place where Jesus was. We hang up our star to remember Jesus' birthday.'

'Thank you for telling me all that,' said Haffertee, politely. 'Now I've solved my star clue. I'm ready for the next one. I must be getting very close to the Happy Christmas.'

Yo finished making the star. She put all the odd bits of cardboard in the waste-paper basket and went proudly downstairs with the shining model. She hung the star right in the middle of the big window in the front room. It looked beautiful.

'You *have* made a lovely star this year,' said Ma. 'I think it's the nicest ever.'

Yo was very pleased. She stood for some time close to the star in the window, and waved to her friends as they went down the road.

That night, when Yo went to bed, she thanked God for all the fun of making things. Then from her bed, she saw something moving in the window. She was rather frightened at first, but then she saw what it was: a star. Not a very good one, but certainly a star.

'Haffertee,' she called. 'Did you put the star in our window?'

'Yes,' he said. 'Howl and I have been working hard all day making stars. We've put one in every window in the house.'

'Every window in the house?' said Yo, in surprise.

'Yes,' said Haffertee. 'Every one. We aren't going to remember Jesus' birthday only in the front room, are we?'

'Er . . . Well . . . No,' said Yo, smiling.

'There's a star in every room,' Haffertee went on firmly. 'We can remember his birthday all over the

34

house now. And he can have any room he likes!'

Yo giggled. She reached inside her pillowcase for the small card with its star picture.

'You may as well have this now,' she said, 'as

you've been making so many stars! Keep it with the others, Christmas Detective, and I'll give you the fourth clue.

> Letters and cards come at Christmas time,
> With love and good wishes too.
> Look at them very carefully –
> They come from your friends to you.'

Haffertee said the words again softly to himself before he went to sleep. Then he knew he wouldn't forget them.

Good Friend Time

With so much going on at Hillside House, Haffertee was glad to find a quiet spot. He was sitting on the mat just inside the front door. No one seemed to come there much at all.

Howl Owl was with him, just sitting and thinking and watching. Howl loved sitting and thinking and watching. He was very good at it.

Suddenly there was a whirr and a plonk and a rattle and the two of them disappeared under a shower of envelopes! Big ones and small ones. Thick ones and thin ones. Brown ones and white ones. There were envelopes everywhere.

Haffertee and Howl were still pushing their way out from under the pile, when they heard several pairs of feet thundering towards them.

'It's the mail,' shouted Yo, and Ma came out from the kitchen.

'Mail,' shouted Chris, and Fran stopped playing her guitar.

'Letters,' shouted Mark, and Pops stopped typing.

The whole family gathered just inside the front door.

Yo picked up all the envelopes as Haffertee and Howl scrambled clear. She began to read out the names written on them: Ma Diamond, Pops Diamond, Fran . . . Chris . . . Howl. One by one she handed them out, and everyone was busy opening the envelopes and looking inside. Then one by one they went off to the kitchen to put the envelopes in a special box. Ma would pin all the new cards up in the kitchen later in the day when she had time.

Haffertee stayed with Howl Owl. Howl had one card, tucked under his wing. He was smiling.

'Well, well!' he said slowly. 'He never forgets!'

Haffertee waited. The Christmas Detective had to know what all these cards were about. Howl just went on looking at his. At last Haffertee could wait no longer.

'What *is* it, Howl?' he asked.

Howl stopped nodding his head and showed his card to Haffertee. On it was a picture of an owl: a most magnificent owl.

'That's Owling,' said Howl, with great pride. 'He is my very best owl friend and he lives up at Hunter's Lodge. He always sends me a picture of himself at Christmas time to remind me of our good friend times together.'

Haffertee thought that was a very nice idea. He felt just a little bit sad that no one had sent him a card. But he didn't say so.

Howl pointed to some writing under the picture. 'Read this Haffertee,' he said.

Haffertee read it out loud.

'To Howl, my very special friend.
A Christmas greeting true.
May all the fun of this good time
Be yours at Christmas too.'

'He wrote it himself,' said Howl proudly. 'He writes a new one every Christmas. And I send him a card, too, to wish him a very Happy Christmas.'

'What a nice idea,' thought Haffertee. 'Excuse me, Howl,' he said politely. 'There's something I want to do.' And he set off upstairs for Diamond Yo's room.

He was glad Yo wasn't there, because he wanted to use her desk. Sitting down on the top, he took some sheets of white paper and began to draw. Once or twice he screwed up a piece of paper into a small ball and dropped it into the waste-paper basket. Then he started to draw again. He tried several times before he was satisfied. It was a picture of himself.

'Now I must colour it,' he muttered to anyone and no one.

He found Yo's colouring pencils and started to colour in his picture. He took great care not to go over the lines. At last it was finished, and he sat back to look at his work. It was a lovely coloured picture of Haffertee Hamster Diamond and he was very pleased with it.

'Now for the poem,' he said. He sat back and closed his eyes. It took a long time and lots of pieces of paper. But at last he was happy. He wrote his poem carefully under the picture.

> This is Jesus' birthday.
> It's a very lovely time.
> And this is a card to tell you
> You're a special friend of mine.
> So here's a coloured picture.
> I did it by myself.
> It will always tell you, 'Hello friend!'
> If you stand it on the shelf.

After that, Haffertee did lots more drawing and lots more writing. He worked hard all afternoon and all evening. When he had finished he felt quite tired but very pleased.

And so were all the Diamond family next morning

when the mail came. Everyone of them had a Haffertee Hamster Christmas card in an envelope. They *were* pleased.

But there was another surprise to come. When everyone had opened their cards there was one envelope left on the mat.

'It's got your name on, Haffertee,' said Yo. 'Open it up!'

Haffertee was so excited, Yo had to help him. Inside was not one, but *three* cards.

The first was a proper Christmas card, made by Yo, with a picture of Ma and Pops and Fran and Chris and Mark and Howl – *and* Yo – on the front.

The second was marked, 'For Haffertee's Very Own Box'. That had a Christmas card picture on it.

And the third one said: 'For the Christmas Detective – Clue Number 5:

Listen to all the carols.
They tell of a baby's birth.
A boy – whose name was Jesus,
Bringing peace on earth.'

Now Haffertee had four pictures and five clues.

That was good. And so were the Haffertee Hamster Diamond Christmas cards. Ma pinned every one of them up in the kitchen that evening. Haffertee *did* feel proud!

Haffertee
and the Music Box

Haffertee was getting ready to go out. Yo had promised he could go with her to sing carols for some older people who lived at the top of the hill. Carols had to be listened to carefully – that was what his clue said. So Haffertee didn't want to be left behind.

There had been a lot of practicing. Mark had been singing with Chris and Fran. All three of them had learned Chris's new carol and they sang it very well. Yo had woken up early once or twice, thinking of the special song she had to sing at church.

Pops had been humming the tune of 'Hark the herald angels' and Ma had been trying to get the high notes right in 'O come all ye faithful.'

Even Howl Owl had been trying out his voice.

Everyone was in a singing mood, and Haffertee was listening carefully to the words.

Then something happened to upset him.

A noisy Music Box arrived.

Haffertee wasn't very sure where he'd come from – upstairs somewhere. But wherever it was . . . he came. He was a long box with black-and-white pieces at one end and some little round knobs at the other. He was all crinkled in the middle.

Most of the time he was quite short but when Ma picked him up he became very long indeed. Ma pulled at him and squeezed him in and twisted him. She put her fingers on the black-and-white pieces at one end and she pressed the knobs at the other. And the box began to sing. Ma and the Music Box got on very well together. And everyone joined in with the singing. It was great fun.

But the Music Box made so much noise that the Christmas Detective couldn't listen to the words. And he didn't like it at all!

So he decided to stop the Music Box from singing!

'I'll stick him together with some glue,' thought Haffertee. 'Then he can't make a sound!'

He made his way to Yo's room and climbed on to her desk. The tube of glue was there, just where he remembered. Haffertee grabbed it round the middle and squeezed. Several drops of glue fell on to the desk.

'Good,' said Haffertee. 'That should take care of him! Now where is that noise-making box?' Downstairs he went, straight to the front room. The Music Box was in the corner, taking a rest.

Haffertee grabbed him and began to pull. There was a loud s-k-w-a-r-k! Haffertee jumped. Yo appeared in the doorway.

44

'Whatever are you doing with my glue?' asked Yo, sternly. She came over to the corner and took the tube away.

'Haffertee!' she said, when she saw what he was doing. 'Haffertee! Were you putting glue on the Music Box? That's not very nice. Why ever do you want to do that?'

Haffertee looked at the floor and shuffled his feet. He was a little bit sorry he'd ever thought of the idea. The rest of the family were standing round now – all waiting for an answer.

'That silly Music Box was making too much noise,' he said. 'If I can't listen to the words, I'll *never* find a Happy Christmas! So I thought if I stuck him together he wouldn't be able to sing any more.'

There was a pause. Then everyone laughed!

'Poor old Haffertee,' Yo said. 'You do take being a Christmas Detective seriously! You'll find the Happy Christmas, don't you worry. But you mustn't glue up the Music Box. We need him for our Christmas carol singing. Come on, now. Let's sing a few more songs before it's time to go.'

So they did. They all sang and sang and sang. And Ma Diamond and the Music Box sang loudest of them all. Haffertee didn't feel much like singing at first. But soon he was singing as merrily as the rest.

When they had finished, Haffertee went over to the Music Box.

'Sorry, Music Box,' he said. 'I promise I'll sing so well tonight you'll be proud of me.'

And the Music Box made a squeaking noise that sounded like . . . 'I'm sure you will.'

Haffertee did sing beautifully that night. And he tried very hard to understand the words. That was the way to find the Happy Christmas.

Secrets

Haffertee found the next clue very quickly, hidden behind the curtain on the window-sill: a little card-picture of the carol singers with the Music Box. And a piece of paper with some words on it. Haffertee could read them easily:

> 'When everyone has secrets
>   And presents to hide away,
>   Remember we're making friends happy
>   For that special Jesus Day.'

The family was out. But the sewing-machine was whirring away at top speed in Ma and Pops' bedroom.

Haffertee pushed open the door and peeped in.

'Oh, it's you, Haffertee,' said Ma. 'Come in and close the door. I was afraid you had Yo with you.'

Haffertee thought that sounded funny, but he didn't say so.

'Can you keep a secret, Haffertee?' Ma went on.

Haffertee pricked up his ears. 'Secret . . . secret . . . That was something else to do with a Happy Christmas.'

'Yes,' he said, eagerly, and shut the door.

Ma beckoned him closer, so that she could pick him up.

'There,' she said, and sat him down in the middle of some lovely soft blue material. She bent down close.

'You see,' she whispered, 'I'm making this dress for Yo for Christmas. I do hope she likes it. It took me such a long time to choose the material. Do you like it, Haffertee?'

Haffertee certainly did. Blue was his favourite colour. But most of all he loved the feel of it around him.

'I think I know just the sort of dress Yo would like,' said Ma.

'Will it be like that one?' asked Haffertee, pointing to Yo's school dress on the chair.

'No, not really,' said Ma. 'That's just to help me make it the right size. You will keep my secret, won't you? Not a word until Yo opens the parcel on Christmas Day.'

Haffertee nodded excitedly. He *did* feel important. Ma had shared *her* secret with him. He moved carefully to the back of the table so that Ma could get on with making the dress. He watched for some time and thought how clever she was to be able to make things like that. She was working very hard on a secret to make Yo happy. And that would make Jesus happy, too. Wasn't that what Yo had said?

The sewing-machine kept starting and stopping. Scissors snipped and snapped and every now and again Ma said, 'Oh!'

After a long time she glanced up at Haffertee.

He was keeping very quiet.

'Oh!' she said, yet again – but a different 'Oh!' this time. Tears were streaming down Haffertee's fluffy hamster pouches and dropping on to the table.

'Why are you sad, Haffertee?' asked Ma, gently.

'I'd like to make a dress for Yo,' he said. '*I* want to give her a surprise for Christmas.'

'Ah!' said Ma. Not 'Oh!' this time, but a very knowing, 'Ah!' 'Ah! Ha!' And she put a sheet of paper down on the table in front of Haffertee. On the paper she put a box of tiny gaily-coloured beads and a tube of glue. Then she fetched a round piece of card with 'Mr Diamond' written on one side and a safety pin fixed on the other.

'Pops wore this badge last week,' said Ma, 'for people to know who he was. He won't need it any more.'

Haffertee had stopped crying now. He was watching and listening carefully, a puzzled look on his face.

Ma went on. 'Yo's Christmas dress will need something bright and pretty on it. Would you like to make her a brooch?'

'Y-e-s,' said Haffertee, doubtfully. 'I would. But I can't.'

'Ah!' said Ma again. 'But you can, my clever little friend.'

Haffertee was surprised. 'I can?' he said.

'Now, you just take those little tiny beads and that tube of glue and you stick those beads all over one side of that card. Cover Pops' name with them.'

Haffertee didn't need telling twice. He was soon up to his paws sorting and sticking tiny coloured beads.

Ma watched and smiled and returned to her own work happily.

Haffertee was really getting on with things. He was choosing the beads very carefully and sticking each one in place. Half an hour later, there was not one tiny piece of white card to be seen. Only bright sparkling beads, making a lovely, lovely pattern. Haffertee held it up in front of him.

'Ma,' said Haffertee excitedly. 'How's this?'

Ma stopped her sewing-machine and looked.

'Why, Haffertee,' she said. 'That is just beautiful.' She took it from him carefully and held it next to the dress material. 'There,' she said. 'It will look lovely pinned to the dress. It will make Yo so happy.'

Haffertee said nothing. He felt all warm and nice inside. 'If I can make someone happy, I can make Jesus happy, too,' said Haffertee. 'Happy Christmas, Yo. Happy birthday, Jesus.' He was day-dreaming.

'Quickly now,' said Ma. 'I can hear the car

coming back. We'll put the brooch in some cotton wool in this box.'

'But where can I hide it?' squeaked Haffertee.

'Look,' said Ma. 'I'll hide it in this drawer. When we are on our own again you can wrap it up in some special Christmas paper and pop it into the Happy Christmas bag under the tree.'

Haffertee was pleased and excited. 'Thank you, Ma,' he said.

'Now,' said Ma, 'you try and keep Yo out of here for ten more minutes.'

Haffertee dashed out, shutting the door behind him. He met Yo on the stairs, and stood in her way.

'What did you buy?' he asked her.

'Oh! Nothing,' said Yo. 'What have *you* been doing?'

'Oh! Nothing,' said Haffertee. 'Nothing at all.' And he dragged her downstairs again.

'Now I know why nobody tells anybody anything at Christmas time,' thought Haffertee. 'Everyone has secrets!'

Howl Owl flew quietly down on to the floor. He was back from his mysterious visit.

'Hello, Howl!' called Haffertee. 'Where have you been?'

'Oh! Nowhere,' said Howl. 'Nowhere at all!'

On the Back of a Moonbeam

Haffertee had had his last clue. Ma had given it him, with his next-to-last picture, of a secret Christmas parcel.

> Before the Day comes Christmas Eve,
> A night of lovely dreams,
> A night to explore the whole wide world
> On the back of the soft moonbeams.

Only another hour or two, and then he would know what a Happy Christmas really was. But tonight he was asleep, dreaming and listening to the moonbeams, sharing their light.

'Would you like to come with us?' they whispered, softly, so softly.

'We can take you anywhere you'd like to go.'

There was only one place in all the world that Haffertee wanted to see tonight, Christmas Eve. He wanted to go to Bethlehem. That was where Jesus was born. Yo had told him.

'Jump on. Jump on, then, and off we'll go. To Bethlehem before you know.'

And Haffertee did. He settled on the back of one

of the moonbeams and they swung up and away into the night sky.

Soon he saw a strange light flickering in the dark. It grew slowly clearer and clearer. There was a bright, shining star, the biggest and loveliest he'd ever seen. It looked as if it was hanging in a window. A great, dark window with no edges.

Haffertee watched as he came closer and closer. And then, right underneath the star he saw a silent village, asleep on the side of a hill. In the middle of the village was an inn – its lights spilling out into the darkness. And behind the inn, a shed. A cowshed.

Haffertee remembered he had seen the place before. The door was open and calling him in. Inside Haffertee could see a glow of light.

A donkey stood quietly near the shed wall. A soft-eyed ox was looking with loving concern at a small wooden manger against the wall. In it was a tiny new-born baby boy, wrapped tight against the cold.

His mother, Mary, sat close by, smiling down at her very first baby.

Joseph, Mary's husband, stood in the shadows by the donkey. His hands were strong and firm. He was a wood-worker.

High in the cobwebbed rafters a white dove cooed a lullaby for the child in the manger.

Jesus lay there, listening.

Haffertee was delighted by what he saw. He went over to the donkey. No need to ask questions, just listen.

'I carried him to Bethlehem,' said the dark brown

54

donkey. 'Mary rode on my back.'

'I let him have my manger,' said the soft-eyed ox.

Haffertee moved over to the wooden manger and looked inside. The baby seemed to be smiling.

Suddenly the light went dim and shadows fell on the straw. Strong men with weathered faces had come into the cowshed. They were all shepherds. They had come running down the hill into the village because

55

of the angels' message. They were silent now, as they saw the baby.

The innkeeper came in, carrying food for Mary and Joseph. 'How kind', thought Haffertee. But no one else took any notice. They were all gazing at the manger and the new-born child. Softly Haffertee began to sing:

> 'Baby born.
> Jesus child.
> Hear the angels sing.
> Baby born.
> God's own style.
> Little Jesus King.'

Haffertee sang and sang and sang. He sang so loudly that he woke Diamond Yo. She turned gently in her bed and reached out to stroke Haffertee's tummy.

'Go to sleep, Haffertee,' she said. 'Go to sleep. Tomorrow is Christmas Day.'

Haffertee Finds his Happy Christmas

Haffertee was awake very early on Christmas Day. Diamond Yo woke him up, squealing with delight and excitement as she looked at all the things in her stocking. Howl Owl was sitting and watching and blinking his eyes, up on his shelf above the door.

'A Happy Christmas,' called Haffertee.

'Happy Christmas,' grunted Howl.

'Many happy returns, Jesus,' said Yo, with a wide smile.

'It's only five o'clock,' called Ma from across the passage. Lights were going on all over the place. The Diamond family was coming to life on Christmas morning. It was very exciting.

But they had to wait until after breakfast to open

the presents. They came out of the big white paper bag under the tree. More excitement and lots of surprises. All the secrets were out at last.

'Now,' said Pops, as the excitement died down a little. 'What about helping Haffertee find a Happy Christmas!'

Haffertee was still wearing his Christmas Detective badge, hanging proudly down on his tummy. 'This,' he thought, 'is what I've been waiting for.'

'I hope you kept those cards safely, Haffertee,' said Pops.

'Yes,' said Haffertee. 'They are all in my Very Own Box.' And he hurried upstairs to get them. Seven clues and . . . one . . . two . . . three . . . four . . . five . . . six cards. The cowshed and the special people: that was one. The angel: that was two. The star, three; the Christmas card, four; the carol singers, five – and the secret Christmas parcel, six.

'There's one more to come,' said Pops, as the Christmas Detective showed him the cards. 'Seven clues and seven cards. Let's see who is first to find it.'

Yo joined in. And so did Chris and Fran and

58

Mark. Haffertee and Howl Owl hunted together. Upstairs and downstairs they went. High and low they looked. Here and there, behind this and behind that.

At last Haffertee spied one edge, peeping out from behind a piece of holly.

'Here it is,' he shouted joyfully, and everyone came running. On the seventh card was a picture of a baby in a manger. 'Little Jesus King,' breathed Haffertee, remembering Christmas Eve and his moonbeam journey to Bethlehem.

Pops put all the cards on the table.

'Now turn them over, Haffertee,' he said.

Haffertee climbed excitedly on to the table. On the back of the cards were big red letters, like the ones on the big white paper bag. One said 'T', another said 'HA', a third said 'IS'. Then there was an 'R', a 'PP', a 'CH' and an 'MAS'. It was very puzzling.

'You sort them out, Yo,' said Pops.

Yo looked at him in surprise at first, but then she decided it wasn't too hard after all. She juggled the letters about on the table until she found the

59

answer. She moved them into place, one by one. Haffertee and Howl gasped.

The letters made the words H A P P C H R I S T M A S! It was Haffertee the Christmas Detective, who noticed there was something missing.

'There's a letter missing!' he shouted, excitedly. 'There's a letter missing!'

'You're right,' said Pops. 'And here it is.' He pulled a rather bigger card out of the big thick book he had been reading and gave it to Haffertee. It was the missing letter.

'Y', said Haffertee.

Yo laughed. 'That's the Y of it all, Haffertee. That's what makes a Happy Christmas. It's what you've been finding out all week.'

Haffertee looked at the smiling faces round the table. He looked at the card, and turned it over. The picture on the other side put everything together.

There was the cowshed with the tiny baby in the manger, the soft-eyed ox, the shepherds and the wise men, the innkeeper, Mary and Joseph and the donkey. In the sky outside was the star and the angel. It was a lovely picture.

When everyone had had a good look at it, Pops opened his book.

'Listen to this,' he said, and he began to read.

It was the story of the birth of little Jesus King.

When he had finished, Yo broke the silence.

'Without Jesus,' she said slowly, 'there would never have been a Happy Christmas.'

Haffertee nodded thoughtfully, and slowly took off his badge. He wanted to ask why the baby was called Jesus *King*. But that question could wait. Just now he was right in the middle of a Happy Christmas!

The
Diamond
Family

Fran   Ma

Diamond Yo
with
Hafferee and
Howl Out

Pops

Mark

Chris.